Virtual Villain

SCOOBY-DOO!

AND THE

Virtual Villain

Written by
James Gelsey

A
LITTLE APPLE
PAPERBACK

SCHOLASTIC INC.

New York Toronto London Auckland Sydney
Mexico City New Delhi Hong Kong Buenos Aires

ISBN 0-439-54603-6

Copyright © 2004 by Hanna-Barbera.
SCOOBY-DOO and all related characters and elements
are trademarks of and © Hanna-Barbera.
CARTOON NETWORK and logo are trademarks of and
© Cartoon Network.
(s04)
Published by Scholastic Inc. All rights reserved.
SCHOLASTIC, LITTLE APPLE, and associated logos are
trademarks and/or registered trademarks of Scholastic Inc.

Designed by Carisa Swenson

12 11 10 9 8 7 6 5 4 3   4 5 6 7 8 9/0

Special thanks to Duendes del Sur for cover and interior illustrations.
Printed in the U.S.A.
First printing, August 2004

Virtual Villain

Chapter 1

"King me, Scooby!" Shaggy called from the back of the Mystery Machine.

Scooby reached over and placed a cardboard crown on Shaggy's head. "Ree-hee-hee-hee-hee," he giggled.

"Very funny, Scooby," Shaggy said. "But using the crown we got at the Royal Burger restaurant was not what I had in mind."

Shaggy picked up one of his red checkers and placed it on top of another. "That's more like it," he said.

Suddenly, all of the checkers flew into the air. So did Shaggy and Scooby.

"Hey! Like, watch it, Freddo!" Shaggy called.

"Sorry, guys," Fred called back. "Guess I took that speed bump a little too fast."

Shaggy and Scooby looked at the jumble of checkers all over the back of the Mystery Machine. Their game was officially over.

"Just as well, Scoob," Shaggy said. "I was going to win anyway."

Scooby sat up straight and shook his head.

"Ruh-uh," he said, pointing to himself.

While the two friends argued, Fred steered

2

the van into a parking space. "Here we are," he announced.

Everyone got out of the van and walked across the parking lot. Shaggy looked up and saw a large banner hanging overhead.

"Welcome to Plonck's Checkers Challenge," Shaggy read. "Man, I still don't see what the big deal is about a checkers tournament."

"The big deal is about who's playing," Daphne said. "Ron Ripsnishes!"

"Gesundheit," Shaggy said.

"What was that for?" asked Velma.

"Like, Daphne just sneezed," Shaggy said.

"No, I didn't," Daphne said. "All I said was that Ron Ripsnishes was playing."

"Ress rou!" Scooby barked.

Velma rolled her eyes. "They think you're sneezing every time you say Ron Ripsn — Ron's last name," Velma said.

"Who is this guy, this Ron Rip-something?" Shaggy asked.

"Ripsnishes," Daphne said.

3

"Gesundheit!" Shaggy said with a laugh. Velma just shook her head.

"He's one of the best checkers players in the world," Fred explained. "But he also doesn't like making public appearances, so this is a very big deal."

"Rey! Rook at rhat!" Scooby said. The gang saw someone dressed as a giant black checker trying to walk inside. But he was too big to fit through the door. He turned sideways, pulled his head, hands, and feet inside the checker costume, and rolled himself into the building.

"What a groovy way to travel," Daphne said.

Once inside the lobby, the gang looked around. Just about everyone seemed to be wearing red-and-black-checkered clothing.

"Man, these outfits are checker-rageous!" Shaggy said. "Now tell me again why we're here."

"To watch Ron Ripsnishes play the most important checkers match of his career," said a man dressed in a three-piece checkered suit. "I'm Sawyer Finn, president of the International Checkers Federation."

Shaggy and Scooby looked at each other and yawned.

"Man, you mean we gave up an afternoon at the malt shop to watch some guy named for a sneeze play checkers?" Shaggy moaned. "I mean, there's not even a snack bar around here."

"The really interesting thing is Ron's opponent," Sawyer Finn continued, ignoring Shaggy.

"Like, who is it?" asked Shaggy.

"It's not a who, it's a what," Mr. Finn said. He pointed to a giant television screen hanging from the ceiling. A green computer-generated image filled the screen.

"Rhoo's rhat?" asked Scooby.

"That is Victor," a female voice said from behind the gang. "And he's going to make Ron Ripsnishes sorry he ever picked up a checker!"

Chapter 2

The gang spun around to face Shelby Chipworth, a young computer programmer.

"Victor stands for Virtual Interactive Checkers Tournament Opponent Response software," Shelby said. "It's a software program I've been working on for years."

"But there have been computer checkers games around forever," Velma said. "What makes yours so special?"

"I'm glad you asked." Shelby smiled. "Follow me."

"Be ready to start in a few minutes, Shelby," Mr. Finn said as he walked away.

The gang followed Shelby over to a table. Shelby took a laptop computer out of her backpack. She opened it up and typed some commands.

"The problem with most computer games is that they can't think like people," Shelby said. "They can only be programmed to follow the rules. They make each move by figuring out all of the possible results from their opponent's moves. They pick the one that's most likely to get them closer to winning."

"So what can Victor do that other games can't?" asked Daphne.

"I programmed Victor with all of the official rules, but I also programmed him to think like his opponents," Shelby said. "Shaggy, make a move."

Shaggy used the mouse to move one of his checkers. Victor appeared on the screen and moved one of his. Shaggy and Victor made two more moves each.

"After three moves, Victor starts thinking

like his opponent," Shelby said. "Check it out."

Shaggy made one more move. Then Victor appeared on the screen again, but before he moved his checker, he stopped.

"Time for a snack," Victor announced in a loud, synthesized voice.

"Zoinks!" Shaggy exclaimed. "Like, that's the coolest — and freakiest — thing I've ever seen!"

Shelby smiled and closed the laptop.

"So you really think Victor can beat Ron Ripsnishes?" Daphne asked.

But before Shaggy and Scooby could say anything, Velma snapped, "Don't say it, guys!"

"I know Victor can beat Ron," Shelby said.

"I can't believe no one's discovered your software yet," Velma said.

"Me neither, and that's why I accepted the challenge," Shelby explained. "I mean, the publicity alone — win or lose — will be great. But I can't pay my bills and expand my software lab with publicity, you know what I mean?"

Shelby finished packing up.

"Good luck, Shelby," Daphne said.

"Thanks," Shelby replied as she disappeared into the checkered crowd.

The gang looked up again at the giant television screen. Victor, the checkers character, smiled down at the crowd and waved.

"I can't put my finger on it, but there's

something about Victor that's kind of creepy," Daphne said.

"It will be interesting to see how Ron Rip-snishes responds to him," Velma said.

"You three keep talking about sneezy guy," Shaggy said. "Scooby and I are going to look for some food."

"Just be careful," Daphne said.

Shaggy smiled. "I don't know what you're worried about, Daph," he said. "These crazy checkers people make Scooby and me seem like the most normal ones here."

"I hate to admit it, but Shaggy's got a point," Velma said. "Just don't be late for the start of the checkers match. They won't let you in once it begins."

Shaggy and Scooby waved and went off to find some food. They walked past a man at a table. He was stuffing potato chips in his mouth as he stared at a laptop computer.

"Like, excuse me," Shaggy said.

Startled, the man tossed his bag of chips into the air.

"Aaah!" he cried, frightening Scooby.

"Rikes!" Scooby yelped, as Shaggy jumped into his arms.

Chapter 3

The man pulled himself together and apologized to Shaggy and Scooby.

"I'm just very tense today," he said. The man wiped his greasy hands on his rumpled suit and turned his attention back to the laptop.

"Sorry to bother you, but we were wondering where you got those potato chips," Shaggy said.

"Oh, I brought these with me," he said. "Whenever I get nervous or upset, I eat potato chips. They help calm me down."

"Man, that's just like me and Scooby." Shaggy nodded. "We like to eat when we're nervous or upset. Or happy. Or tired. Or bored. Or pretty much any time at all."

"Reah," Scooby agreed.

"So, like, do you have any more?" Shaggy asked.

But the man didn't answer. He was lost in thought again.

"I think this guy's a few chips short of a bag," Shaggy whispered to Scooby. "Let's get out of here."

As Shaggy and Scooby tiptoed away, the man called after them. "Just a minute!" he said. "I'm sorry for the way I'm acting. Business hasn't been going so well for me. It looks like a major investment I made has turned sour." He motioned to the laptop, where Shaggy and Scooby could see a bunch of numbers on the screen.

"Like, that's too bad," Shaggy said.

The man nodded sadly. "I invested too much, too quickly," he moaned. "And with this checkers competition, I may have to declare bankruptcy."

Shaggy and Scooby looked at each other with puzzled expressions.

"Like, what do you have to do with the checkers competition?" asked Shaggy.

The man glanced at Shaggy and Scooby and smiled. "I'm Everett Plonck," he said, "the sponsor of this event. And the one who put up the one million dollars for the gold trophy."

Shaggy's eyes nearly popped out of their sockets. "Zoinks!" he exclaimed. "That's a lot of potato chips!"

"Rand Rooby racks!" Scooby added.

The man reached into his computer bag and pulled out a travel-size checkers set and a well-thumbed book.

"I got this checkers set and official rule book when I was seven years old," he said. "I've loved the game all my life. And I always dreamed about being part of something like this." He picked up the tiny checkers and squeezed them in his hand. "I'd hate to see my dreams go down the drain like this. I don't know what to do."

Everett Plonck put the checkers set back into his bag. Then he took out another bag of potato chips and handed it to Shaggy.

"Here you go," Everett said. "Thanks for listening."

Scooby's eyes lit up at the sight of the bag. He grabbed it away from Shaggy and opened it.

"You're welcome," Shaggy said as Everett Plonck packed up his things and sadly walked away. "Hey, save some of those for me, Scoob!"

The two of them munched on the chips as Fred, Daphne, and Velma walked over.

"Looks like you two managed to find a snack," Velma said.

"Yeah, and we also found the Plonck in Plonck's Checkers Challenge," Shaggy replied. He told the others about his and Scooby's encounter with Everett Plonck.

"I sure hope things work out for him," Daphne said.

Someone in the crowd shouted, "He's here! He's here!"

The crowd surged toward the front doors and formed an aisle on either side of a red carpet.

"Sounds like Ron Ripsnishes has arrived," Velma said.

Chapter 4

"Let's see if we can get a closer look," Fred said. He started toward the crowd, but Velma had a better idea.

"Hold on, Fred, let's wait over there," she said. She pointed to a plain-looking door. "This is the door that leads to the dressing rooms and backstage area. If we wait behind those palm trees next to the door, we'll be able to see him up close, away from the crowds."

The gang stepped behind the row of potted palms and waited. A moment later, the crowd started cheering and waving. In walked a tall, athletic-looking man dressed in a blue suit. Next to him walked an older man in tan pants and a green shirt. The older man held something tightly against his chest. He kept his eyes on the carpet as he walked.

At the end of the red carpet, a wall of security guards held the crowd back. The two men walked toward the door and the palm trees. Velma noticed that the older man was holding a laptop computer.

"I don't care how many times you've won, Ron," the man in the suit said. "Victor is ten times — no, a million times — smarter than those other computer checkers games you've been playing. You've got to take this challenge seriously."

"Don't tell me what I need to do," the older man replied. "I've been winning checkers championships since before the computer was even invented."

The man in the suit shook his head. "Ron, I'm telling you as your manager," he began, "if you don't win this thing, you're done. No one will give you the time of day anymore. And the fact that you don't even acknowledge your fans doesn't help."

One of the guards opened the door.

"I may be old, but I've still got some tricks up my sleeve," Ron Ripsnishes said with a sly smile. "Don't worry about me."

The two men disappeared down the hallway as the door shut behind them. A security guard remained outside the door.

Fred, Velma, and Daphne stepped out from behind the palm trees.

"Sounds like this could be a very interesting checkers match after all," Velma said.

"And if we want good seats, we'd better get inside now," Fred said. "People have already started going in."

They noticed that crowds were moving through the main doors into the auditorium.

"Come on, Shaggy! Let's go, Scooby," Daphne called.

Shaggy and Scooby didn't answer. Fred looked behind the palm trees.

"They're gone," Fred said.

"Oh, no," Daphne moaned. "What do you think they're up to?"

"Just bringing you a little checkers cheer," Shaggy announced. Fred, Daphne, and Velma turned around.

"Shaggy! Scooby! What are you wearing?" Velma asked.

The two of them were decked out in full checkers gear. Shaggy wore a checkered vest over his shirt and a wide-brimmed hat in the shape of giant checker. Scooby wore a checkered shirt.

"Scoob and I figured if you can't beat 'em, join 'em," he said. "Plus, we found out that if you're wearing checkers stuff you can get free snacks."

"Rhese are ror rou," Scooby said.

He handed Daphne a checkered head-band. Fred got a checkered ascot for around his neck. And for Velma, there was a check-ered vest to wear over her sweater.

"Thanks, fellas," Daphne said. "Now can we go inside?"

"Like, lead the way," Shaggy said.

The gang got in line and followed every-one else into the auditorium.

Chapter 5

Fred, Daphne, Velma, Shaggy, and Scooby walked into the large auditorium and stopped.

"Gee, where is everybody?" Daphne wondered. "The lobby seemed so crowded."

Fred and Velma looked around. The checkers fans filled the first ten rows, but the rest of the auditorium was largely empty.

"I thought this 'man versus machine' challenge would have attracted more people," Velma said.

"So did I," Fred agreed.

"But man, what they lack in numbers they

more than make up for in, like, weirdness," Shaggy added.

The gang checked their tickets and then decided to sit in some empty seats closer to the stage.

"We can always move if we have to," Daphne reasoned. They sat down as the lights in the auditorium dimmed. Sawyer Finn stepped out onto the stage.

"Good afternoon, ladies and gentlemen," he said. "My name is Sawyer Finn, and as

president of the International Checkers Federation, I'd like to welcome you to this once-in-a-lifetime event."

A clicking sound filled the auditorium.

"Man, who let the crickets in here?" Shaggy asked.

"Those aren't crickets," Fred said. "It's the audience clicking checkers together. I guess that's how they applaud at these things."

"Now, without further ado, let's get things started," Mr. Finn announced. "Please give a warm checkers cheer to grand master Ron Ripsnishes and his challenger, the Virtual Interactive Checkers Tournament Opponent Response software, known as Victor."

There was more clicking as the lights came up to reveal a table in the center of the stage. Three large television screens hovered over the table. The screen on the right contained a close-up of Ron Ripsnishes sitting at the table. The center screen provided a look at the checker board. And the screen on

the left featured Victor's computer-generated image. The checkers character waved to everyone in the crowd. A beautiful golden trophy stood on a pedestal off to the side.

"The contestants flipped a coin, and Victor won," Mr. Finn explained in a quiet voice. "Victor has decided to let Ron Ripsnishes move first. Once the game begins, no talking or flash photography, please."

Everyone waited for Ron Ripsnishes to make his first move.

Ron slid one of his checkers forward.

"Ah, the Bubinsky opening," muttered someone in the audience.

Before Victor could make his first move, a strange rumbling filled the auditorium. The checkers on the large television screen began to vibrate slightly and then dance around the board.

The rumbling grew louder until people were covering their ears. There was a flash of light and a loud explosion, followed by complete darkness. As the emergency lights flickered on, Fred thought he saw something standing on the stage.

"What's that?" he asked, pointing to the shadowy figure.

As the lights brightened, everyone saw exactly who it was.

"Zoinks!" Shaggy exclaimed. "It's Victor!"

"Rikes!" Scooby yelped as he dived under his seat.

The computer checkers player stood on

the stage as real as could be. "Give it up for grand master Victor!" he roared.

The people in the audience couldn't believe their eyes. Frightened, many of them jumped out of their seats and ran up the aisles.

"That's right, run! Run and tell the world I am here!" Victor announced in a booming voice. He strode across the stage and grabbed the golden trophy.

"I'll be happy to hold on to this," he said. "Unless anyone cares to challenge me, that is!" Victor waved his left hand at the audience. Suddenly, a shower of checkers fell from the ceiling into the stands. The audience couldn't leave the auditorium fast enough.

As Victor laughed, the emergency lights went off and threw everything back into darkness. A moment later, the regular lights came back on. The stage was empty, as was the rest of the auditorium.

"Jinkies!" Velma exclaimed. "I can't believe Victor came to life and stole the trophy!"

"And Ron Ripsnishes!" Daphne added. "Look!"

Everyone noticed Ron's chair lying on its side.

"Looks to me like we've got a real mystery on our hands," Fred said. "Time to get to work!"

Chapter 6

The gang made its way onto the stage.

"Look around for anything that seems out of place," Fred said.

"Great idea, Fred," Shaggy said. "C'mon, Scoob, let's get out of this place."

Shaggy and Scooby started to walk off stage.

"Not so fast you two," Daphne called. "We have to work together if we're going to solve this mystery."

"I'll look around here with Shaggy and Scooby," Velma offered.

"Great, Velma," Fred said. "Daphne and I

will see if there's anything suspicious back-stage."

Scooby sniffed around the checkers table and sat in one of the chairs. Shaggy picked up Ron's chair and sat down. He studied the board for a moment and then slid one of the checkers to an adjacent square. As he lifted his finger, an-other checker moved by itself.

"Zoinks!" Shaggy cried.

Shaggy and Scooby sprang away from the table and landed in front of Velma.

"What is it, you two?" she asked. "You look like you've seen a ghost."

"Ghost checkers is more like it," Shaggy said.

He told Velma how the checker had

moved by itself. Curious, Velma examined the table. Then she peered beneath it.

"Aha!" she said. "Just as I suspected."

"Don't tell me you've found the checkers ghost," Shaggy said.

"No, just this," she replied.

She held out a small black box with an antenna on it. Three small red lights blinked on and off.

"This is a wireless remote control receiver," Velma said. "It must have been hooked up to the checkers table to allow Victor's checkers to move."

"I thought Victor was a computer program," Shaggy said. "Like, how does a computer program make real checkers move?"

"Shelby Chipworth probably designed a

program that translated Victor's computer moves into a wireless signal," Velma explained. "I'll bet the checker board and checkers are magnetized so the pieces could slide according to the computer's instructions."

Shaggy let out a deep breath. "Man, I'm glad you found that clue," he said. "I guess that means Shelby Chipworth is guilty and we can all go home now. Let's go for a pizza, Scooby."

"Rokay!" Scooby answered.

"Sorry, Shaggy, but this isn't a clue," Velma said. "This had to be installed long before Victor showed up this afternoon. Here's the real clue. I found it on the other side of the stage."

Velma held up a black oval object that fit neatly in the palm of her hand. It had a small ball sticking out of the bottom.

"Is that, like, a computer mouse?" asked Shaggy.

"A wireless computer mouse, to be precise," Velma answered. "Just like one you'd use with a laptop computer."

Fred and Daphne appeared behind Velma.

"A computer someone could use to override the lights and sound system," Fred said.

"So, like, if we find the computer, we'll find the culprit and we can get out of here," Shaggy said.

Daphne shook her head. "Sorry, Shaggy,

but it won't be that easy," she said. "Fred and I looked everywhere backstage and couldn't find any sign of a laptop. I'm afraid there's only one way we're going to solve this mystery."

"By finding more clues," Velma and Fred said together.

"I was afraid of that," moaned Shaggy.

Chapter 7

$\int$haggy had an idea. "Scooby and I will see if we can find anything out in the lobby," he offered.

"Ruh?" Scooby said, taken by surprise.

"Good idea, Shaggy," Daphne said. "I'm proud of you for wanting to help out."

Shaggy jumped off the stage. "Well, are you coming, Scoob?" he asked, winking at Scooby. "I really need your help if I'm going to find anything out in the lobby."

Shaggy and Scooby ran up the aisle and into the lobby.

"Good luck finding clues!" Daphne called.

Once they were out in the lobby, Shaggy turned to Scooby. "You'll notice, Scooby, that I never said anything about finding *clues*," Shaggy said to his friend. "Now, food, that's another story."

Scooby smiled and slapped Shaggy on the back. "Rood roy!" he said.

Shaggy and Scooby walked through the abandoned lobby.

"It's kind of creepy out here all alone," Shaggy said. "I never thought I'd say it, but I kinda miss those checkers people. They may have been strange, but at least they were people, and not some computer program gone crazy."

"Your move!" a strange voice called.

Shaggy and Scooby stopped in their tracks.

"Like, did you hear something, Scooby?" asked Shaggy.

"Rid rou?" asked Scooby.

"I did if you did," Shaggy answered.

"Re roo," Scooby said.

They looked around, but didn't see anything.

"I guess it's in our imaginations," Shaggy
said.

He and Scooby started walking toward
one of the souvenir shops.

"I said that it's your move!"

Shaggy and Scooby stopped.

"Like, Fred? Velma? Daphne?" Shaggy
called in a creaky voice. "Is that you?"

"Guess again!"

Shaggy and Scooby slowly turned around and came face-to-face with Victor!

"Rikes!" Scooby yelped.

"Zoinks!" Shaggy cried. They turned and bumped into each other. But they quickly recovered and raced away.

"Relp! Relp!" Scooby barked.

Victor chased Shaggy and Scooby all over the lobby. Shaggy and Scooby dove behind the row of potted palm trees to hide.

"Stay quiet, Scooby, and don't move a whisker," Shaggy whispered.

A few moments later, Shaggy and Scooby slowly stood up. They carefully parted the palm leaves and poked their heads out.

"Ahhh!" shrieked Daphne.

"Ahhh!"

cried Shaggy and Scooby. They collapsed against each other, lost their balance, and fell on the floor, knocking down two of the potted palms.

Daphne, Fred, and Velma stood over Shaggy and Scooby.

Shaggy looked up at Daphne. "Sorry to scare you, Daph, but we thought you were Victor," he explained. "He was just chasing us around the lobby."

"That's not all he was doing," Fred said. "Look. He dropped something."

Velma picked up a small book and looked at the title. *The Official Checkers Rule Book,* authorized by the International Checkers Federation," she read.

"Sounds like another clue to me," Daphne said. "Good work, fellas."

"Ranksh," Scooby said, his mouth full of food.

"Hey! What are you eating?" Shaggy asked.

Scooby smiled and pointed to something yellow at the base of one of the potted palms.

Shaggy reached down and plunged his hand into the yellow object. He came up with a handful of potato chips.

"Just what the detective ordered!" Shaggy announced happily as he stuffed the potato chips into his mouth.

Fred's, Daphne's, and Velma's eyes lit up.

"That's it!" Velma said. "The final clue!"

"Which means it's time to set a trap," Fred said. "Gather 'round, gang. I've got an idea that will make our computer villain get with *our* program."

Chapter 8

"Victor's already taken the golden trophy," Fred said. "So there's only one thing that can lure him back here."

"Like, a female computer checkers game come to life?" asked Shaggy.

"No, Shaggy," Daphne said. "Victor believes he is the best checkers player in the world."

"So we have to convince him otherwise," Fred said.

"Or rather, you do," Velma added.

"In the words of my pal Scooby," Shaggy said, "ruh?"

Fred, Daphne, and Velma smiled.

"It's easy, Shaggy," Daphne said. "All you have to do is sit at the table on the stage and play checkers."

"Ro roblem," Scooby said.

Shaggy glared at his friend. "Like, easy for you to say," Shaggy moaned. "You don't have to come face-to-face with that cyber-creep."

"He's right, Scooby," Fred said. "All *you* have to do is get Victor to chase you up the aisle and out into the lobby."

"That's where we'll be waiting to capture Victor," Velma said.

"Like, no problem, right, Scooby?" Shaggy said with a smile.

Scooby shook his head. "Ro ray," he barked.

Daphne reached into her pocket. "Maybe a Scooby Snack will change your mind?" she said, smiling. She tossed the treat into the air. Scooby's eyes zeroed in on it and followed its flight up, then down. At the last moment, he stuck his paw out and caught the Scooby Snack just before it hit the floor.

"Rummy!" he said, flicking the treat into his mouth.

"Velma, Daphne, let's go grab one of the big banners off the wall to toss over Victor," Fred said. "Shaggy and Scooby, you two get into position."

Fred, Velma, and Daphne left the auditorium. Shaggy and Scooby climbed up onstage. They faced each other across the checkers table.

"How about it, Scoob?" asked Shaggy. "Ready for a rematch?"

"Rou ret!" answered Scooby.

They sat down at the table. Shaggy clasped his fingers together and stretched them out in front of him. *POP POP POP POP POP POP*! went his knuckles.

Scooby put his paws together and did the same thing. *PUP PUP PUP PUP PUP PUP!* went his knuckles.

Just as Shaggy was about to make his first move, other sounds filled the room.

CRICK CRACK PLOP SPLAT BOOOOOM BUUUURRRRRRP!

Shaggy looked up and started shaking. "Man, tell me that sound came from you, Scooby," he whined.

Scooby slowly shook his head. "Rot re," he said.

Shaggy swallowed hard. "Then I guess it's, like, you know who," he whispered.

"You mean me?" asked Victor from behind Scooby. "Please, call me Vic!"

"Zoinks!" Shaggy cried, diving under the table. "Go, Scooby, go!"

"Rikes!" Scooby cried as he jumped up. Victor reached out to grab Scooby, but Scooby ducked down and jumped off the stage.

"So you wanted to play a game of checkers with Victor in the house?" the computer monster shouted. His voice echoed through the auditorium. "No one plays until Victor plays!"

The villain chased Scooby up the aisle. Shaggy leaped off stage and raced up another aisle. Fred, Daphne, and Velma stood outside the door, ready to throw the banner over Victor as soon as he ran out.

Scooby burst through the door — but it was the wrong one! He ran across the lobby with Victor close behind. Shaggy burst through the door where Fred, Daphne, and

Velma stood. In an instant, he was wrapped up in the giant banner.

"Like, now I know what an enchilada feels like," his muffled voice said.

Victor chased Scooby through the lobby. Scooby disappeared into one of the gift shops. Victor followed him and, a moment later, ran out screaming.

Scooby rolled through the lobby dressed in a giant checker costume. He was right on Victor's heels.

"Help!" Victor cried.

As Shaggy climbed out of the banner, Fred, Daphne, and Velma knocked down the potted palms, blocking Victor's path. Victor tripped on the palm trees and landed with a

splat in the middle of the banner. Scooby rolled on over and wobbled to a stop at the edge of the banner.

"Like, good work, Scoob," Shaggy said, giving Scooby a pat on the back. Scooby tumbled over and squashed Victor beneath the giant checker costume.

"Now that gives new meaning to the phrase 'king me,'" Daphne said.

Chapter 9

After the gang helped Scooby up and out of his costume, they turned their attention to Victor.

"Ohhh, my aching back," he muttered.

"That's the first time I've ever heard a computer program complain about its back," Sawyer Finn said as he walked over. "By the way, the police should be here any minute."

"That'll give us plenty of time to see who's behind this mystery," Velma said. "Would you care to do the honors, Mr. Finn?"

Sawyer Finn leaned over and removed Victor's mask.

"Everett Plonck!" he exclaimed.

Everett sighed deeply. He hung his head in shame.

"Just as we suspected," Velma said.

Sawyer Finn looked at the gang with a puzzled expression on his face. "How in the world could you have known?" he asked.

"Well, it wasn't easy," Daphne said. "But after finding a few clues, we were able to figure it out."

Velma showed Mr. Finn the computer mouse.

"This was our first clue," she said. "And it told us that whoever was dressing up as Victor had access to a laptop. We remembered that Shelby Chipworth, Ron Ripsnishes —"

"Gesundheit," Shaggy said.

"— and Everett Plonck all had laptops with them when they arrived here," she continued.

"And just as important, each of them also had a motive for wanting to get their hands on that trophy," Fred added.

"So how did you go from the three of them down to Everett Plonck?" asked Mr. Finn.

"These two other clues," Daphne said. "Victor dropped this official checkers rule book, which told us that he needed a little help with the game."

"Mr. Plonck showed Shaggy and Scooby a book just like this one," Fred said.

Just then, Shelby Chipworth approached. "And I have one just like it that I used to help write the program," she said.

"What's more, we concluded there was no way Ron Ripsnishes would ever need one of these, considering how good he is at the game," Velma said.

"Sounds like you kids really have a nose for clues," Mr. Finn said with a smile.

"Thanks, Mr. Finn, but it was Scooby's stomach that really clinched it for us," Daphne said. She showed everyone the potato chip bag Scooby found in the potted palm trees.

"Only one suspect was eating potato chips," Fred said. "And once we realized who it was, we were ready to set the trap."

All eyes turned to Everett Plonck.

"But why, Everett?" asked Mr. Finn.

"I was almost bankrupt!" Everett cried. "I couldn't just sit around and watch that golden trophy slip away like that! I was going to use the gold in the trophy to rebuild my company. And I would have gotten away with it — except those meddling kids and their potato-chip munching mutt got in the way."

Sawyer Finn chuckled softly to himself and shook his head.

"Everett, I hate to tell you this," he began, "but all you would have gotten away with was a giant checker made of clay. The real gold trophy has been in my safe since you brought it in this morning."

Everett's face fell. As the police arrived and helped Everett to his feet, Ron Ripsnishes poked his head out from behind a broom closet door.

"Is it safe to come out now?" he asked.

"Yes, it's safe, Ron," Mr. Finn said.

"Mr. Ripsnishes!" Daphne said. "We thought Victor kidnapped you."

"As soon as he showed up, I ran offstage and hid in this broom closet," he explained. "Now how about that game of checkers?"

Ron Ripsnishes stepped out of the broom closet and froze in his tracks. "My word, that's the biggest checker

I've ever seen," he said, looking at Scooby in the checker costume.

"That's no checker," Shaggy said. "That's my pal!"

"Rcooby-Rooby-Roo!" Scooby cheered.